DAVID MORTIMORE BAXTER

Excuses!

by Karen Tayleur

illustrated by Brann Garvey

Librarian Reviewer
Kathleen Baxter
Children's Literature Consultant
formerly with Anoka County Library, MN
BA College of Saint Catherine, St. Paul, MN
MA in Library Science, University of Minnesota

Reading Consultant
Elizabeth Stedem
Educator/Consultant, Colorado Springs, CO
MA in Elementary Education, University of Denver, CO

STONE ARCH BOOKS
Minneapolis   San Diego

First published in the United States in 2007
by Stone Arch Books, A Capstone Imprint
1710 Roe Crest Drive,
North Mankato, Minnesota 56003.
www.capstonepub.com

Published by arrangement with Black Dog Books.

Library of Congress Cataloging-in-Publication Data
Tayleur, Karen.
    Excuses!: Survive and Succeed with David Mortimore Baxter / by Karen
Tayleur; illustrated by Brann Garvey.
        p. cm. — (David Mortimore Baxter)
    Summary: Young David Mortimore Baxter, who knows how to stay out of
trouble, shares excuses for avoiding chores, bullies, homework, and vegetarian
dinners.
    ISBN-13: 978-1-59889-073-0 (hardcover)
    ISBN-10: 1-59889-073-5 (hardcover)
    ISBN-13: 978-1-59889-205-5 (paperback)
    ISBN-10: 1-59889-205-3 (paperback)
    [1. Excuses—Fiction. 2. Humorous stories.] I. Garvey, Brann, ill. II. Title. III.
Title: Survive and Succeed with David Mortimore Baxter. IV. Series: Tayleur, Karen.
David Mortimore Baxter.
PZ7.T21149Ex 2007
[Fic]—dc22   2006005073

Art Director: Heather Kindseth
Graphic Designer: Kay Fraser

Photo Credits
Delaney Photography, cover

Printed in the USA.
9965R

Table of Contents

CHAPTER 1

THINGS YOU SHOULD KNOW

If you didn't read Liar! (my last book), then there'll be people in this book who you haven't met before.

That's okay, though. If you didn't read Liar, you can still understand what's going on in this book.

But if I mention that Boris used my head as a pillow, you might wonder if Boris was my dad. And then you might think my dad was kind of strange. But, you see, Boris is **my dog**. Actually, if I said that Boris used my head as a pillow, you might think Boris is kind of strange anyway. And you'd be right.

So I've thought up a **list of names** that you might need to know. Just in case I talk about them in this book.

Boris

Boris is my really lazy dog. He's not just one type of dog. He's more like a mix of a lot of different kinds of dogs. Boris sleeps most of the day. He doesn't like walks. He does like scraps from the table.

Joe Pagnopolous  (pag-nop-a-lus)

Joe is my best friend. He and I belong to a secret club that has no name. (That's because we can't decide on one.) Joe's parents own a video store. Maybe that's why he's so crazy about acting. Joe is always pretending to be his favorite movie character — even at school. I never know who he is going to be next. He has no brothers or sisters. He is the LUCKIEST kid in the WORLD.

Bec Trigg ———→

Bec is my other best friend. We met in the playground when we were really, really young. Some big kid took my ball and Bec got it back for me. She is another member of the SECRET CLUB. She is the keeper of The Book — the official Secret Club Book that goes to official Secret Club meetings.

Bec lives with her mom and sister in an apartment. Bec is good at drawing and throwing spitballs and running fast. **Sometimes I forget she is a girl.**

Ralph

Ralph is a **rat.** No, really. He is Bec's pet rat and he hangs around in her pocket when she's not at school. Ralph's favorite game is peek-a-boo. Ralph upset this year's school play for Rose Thornton, but that's another story.

Rose Thornton

Mom says I'm not allowed to hate people. I really, really, really don't like Rose Thornton. Rose thinks she's so cool. She's always going on about the famous people her mom meets as a PR person. (I'm not sure what PR stands for. Pretty Rude? Purple Ruler? Anyway, it's some kind of job.) Rose hangs around with a group of friends I call the GIGGLING GANG — the **GG's** for short. Rose really, really, really doesn't like me either.

Victor Sneddon

Victor is the school **bully** and just happens to be Rose's cousin.

The only time I've seen him smile is when he is going to do something mean. Then he smiles a lot. Victor and I were almost friends for five minutes one day because of some buried treasure. I still stay out of his way, though.

Ms. Stacey

Ms. Stacey is our teacher at school. She's okay, but she can get mad pretty quickly. Sometimes she has a sense of humor. She is a really big fan of Smashing Smorgan, the wrestler.

Dad

Dad just kind of hangs around. When he goes to work, he's in charge. But when he comes home, he doesn't know what's going on. When I ask Dad if I can have a cookie right before dinner, he'll say, "Of course," even though everyone knows you're not allowed to have anything to eat right before dinner. When Dad's MAD at you, he gets *really quiet*. He makes you feel really bad. I'd rather have Mom yell at me.

MOM

Mom is Mom. My friends really like her. At home she pretends to be really nice and fair. But she's not. She makes me take a shower and make my bed every day. She makes me be nice to my little brother. She also makes some really strange meals, like **veggie loaf**, that we have to eat. (Sometimes I slip mine **under the table** to Boris.) Other than that, she's okay.

Harry

My little brother. What can I say? He can't help it that he's my little brother. Maybe he hates that I was born before he was. But that wasn't my fault. Anyway, Harry acts like his main reason for living is to **annoy** me. He does a really good job.

Zoe

Zoe is my sister and she's the oldest kid in our family. Zoe and I used to get along okay, but then she changed and started wearing dresses and makeup.

She walks around like she's too cool for school. She spends a lot of time in her bedroom. I'd like to go in her bedroom one day and find out what's so interesting in there. I just need to figure out how to UNLOCK her DOOR.

Gran

Old people are supposed to be nice. They always are in books, anyway. Gran is really old and not really nice. She's always angry about something I've done or haven't done. She has **three whiskers** on her **chin —**
really! Sometimes I can't help staring at them. Then I get into trouble for staring.

Mr. McCafferty

Mr. McCafferty is our **neighbor.** Mr. McCafferty knows everything that goes on in our neighborhood. Sometimes he knows before it even happens. He spends a lot of time talking to my mom about me. He likes watching medical shows on TV and he likes his cat, **Mr. Figgins.** He really, really, really doesn't like Boris or me.

CHAPTER 2

I've been around long enough to figure out a few things.

1. that my dog Boris is **never going to win a dog show contest**

2. that **tuna** and **jam do not** make a good sandwich

3. that it's *VERY IMPORTANT* to have a few excuses around for emergencies

Adults are always talking about the good old days when they were kids. How going to school is way more fun than going to work. How being a kid was way easier than being an adult. How kids have it better.

Are they kidding?

There must be a *FORGET BUTTON* that gets pushed when you turn into an adult. I know it will never happen to me.

There is no way I am going to forget how hard it is to be a kid. It seems like everyone is in charge of your life, everyone but you. When I grow up I'm looking forward to being in charge of my own life. I'll go to bed when I want to. I'll get up when I want to. I'll eat **ice cream** and **chips** for dinner if I want to. I won't make my bed, ever.

My mom has this book called **"1001 Handy Hints for Homemakers."** She got it from Dad for her last birthday. She didn't seem too happy when he gave it to her, but it got me thinking that there should be a handy hints book for kids. We'd call it **"1001 Exciting Excuses for Kids."**

I went to the library and asked the librarian if there was a book like that. She told me to search for it on the computer. After about **fifty million hours,** I realized there was no book of exciting excuses for kids. I told the librarian. She said she already knew there wasn't.

So I went home and decided I should write this book. After I finished writing it, I realized that I didn't have 1001 excuses. So I had to change the title of the book, but the idea is still the same. This is a SURVIVAL BOOK for kids.

I read somewhere that kids need to use an excuse every 11.5 minutes. (Actually, I just made that up, but it sounds about right.) So get reading before the next 11.5 minutes come around!

This is my official disclaimer. Bec said I need to put this in the book so I don't get put it jail. So here goes. These excuses are only to be used at your own risk. Some of them are for kids, and some for adults. And some might even be illegal in your town (like Mrs. P.'s excuse to the police on page 62). So don't say I didn't warn you. Thank you.

CHAPTER 3

EXCUSES FOR HOME

At home, **Mom is in charge**. At school there are a bunch of people in charge, but at home there's just Mom. Mom has eyes in the back of her head. I've never seen them, but I know she has them. She can be in a totally different room, but she will know that I'm in the kitchen drinking out of the juice carton from the fridge.

"David Mortimore Baxter! Pour that juice in a glass," she'll yell to me.

Then there's my sister, Zoe, who likes to tell on me whenever possible. And my little brother, Harry, who just snoops around after me, like a bloodhound.

"Guess what David did, Mom," he likes to call out. If I haven't done anything wrong, sometimes he'll make something up. And the worst part is, sometimes Mom believes him.

Then there's Gran, who gets mad about everything I do, like eating with my mouth open.

And there's Mr. McCafferty, who's just waiting for me to do something wrong so he can call Mom about it. "*I'm sorry to have to call you about this, Mrs. Baxter,*" he'll say. Actually, he's not really sorry.

That just leaves Dad and Boris. They leave me alone.

That's home. You can see why I need **a whole book of excuses** just to keep myself out of trouble. Sometimes the excuses work, sometimes they don't. Sometimes it depends who you use them on. I hope some of these work for you.

Table Manners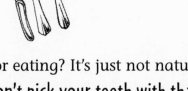

Who invented rules for eating? It's just not natural. A lion wouldn't say, **"Don't pick your teeth with that leg bone, dear."**

Eating is about getting **energy** into our bodies. It's about survival. It's not about whether we chew with our mouths open. Or whether our elbows are on the table. Or if we say PLEASE and THANK YOU.

In our house, eating a meal is a **big deal.**
Someone has to set the table, someone has to get the
drinks ready, and when we're finished, someone has to
clear the dishes. I even have to wash my hands before
I come to the table.

Then we all have to sit down to eat **at the same
time.** Then Dad asks us about our day. And then
when we answer, Mom gets upset at us for talking
with our mouths full.

On Sundays, we have a **big Sunday** lunch. My
friends Bec and Joe usually come over. And Gran is
always there for Sunday lunch too. If you think my
Mom is bad, you should meet Gran. She finds lots of
things to pick on. I try to eat my lunch really fast so I
can leave the table. Then she picks on me for eating
too fast.

I HATE MEAL TIMES.

Here are some excuses I use for them.

1. Not Eating — Have a Cold

Mom: David, close your mouth when you eat.

David: I can't. I've got a cold.

[Then **sniff** loudly. If you think you can get away with a fake sneeze, try it. Make sure you don't have food in your mouth at the same time.]

2. Not Eating — Starving People

Mom: David, please eat your veggie loaf. It's getting cold.

David: I can't, Mom. I just keep thinking about all the starving people in the world who are missing out on such a great meal.

[This one worked for my sister, but didn't work for me.]

3. Elbows on Table — Balancing

Gran: Get your elbows off the table, boy.

David: But it helps me 𝐵𝒜𝐿𝒜𝒩𝒞𝐸, Gran.

[Then take your elbows off the table and wobble in your chair like you might fall over. Be careful not to fall over in your chair, because then you'll really be in trouble.]

4. Gulping Food — Tastes Good

Gran: Don't gulp your food, boy. You should chew it **42** times before swallowing.

David: I can't help eating fast, Gran. **This food is just too good.**

[The good thing about this excuse is Gran can't disagree with me, and I score points with Mom for saying her cooking is good. I've used this a lot and it's worked every time.]

5. Not Eating — Too Good to Eat

Mom: David, you're not eating. Don't you like my new veggie loaf?

David: Mom, I can honestly say that this new loaf is incredible. **I'm saving some for later.**

[This excuse is only half a lie. I looked up "incredible" in the dictionary and it says "impossible to believe." Mom's veggie slice is incredible — incredibly bad! So it isn't completely lying. And I **was** saving some for later. I just forgot to mention that I was saving it for the dog.]

6. Using Hands at Dinner Table — Saving Dishes

Mom: David, stop using your hands and use your knife and fork.

David: But Mom, I'm just making it **easier to wash the dishes.**

[This one depends on what kind of mood Mom is in. She either laughs and makes me use my knife and fork or she gets mad at me for being rude and makes me use my knife and fork.]

7. Washing Dishes — Rare Skin Disease

Mom: Come and wash the dishes please, David.

David: The school nurse said this rash on my hands is a rare skin disease. She said I should avoid washing dishes for at least a month. Even drying dishes can make it worse.

Mom: What rash?

David: Well, of course you can't see it right now — I'm not anywhere near dish soap.

[This one's for after meal times.]

Room For Improvement

Mom has this thing about **my bedroom.** It's like she's expecting a photographer from *Better Homes and Gardens* to stop by any time. The thing is, it's **my bedroom.** If I don't think it's messy, I don't see why it should bother her.

One day I put a sign on my door. It said **"Keep Out. Private Property!"**

Most mothers would pull the sign down or just ignore it. But not my mom. The next thing I knew, she had shoved a piece of paper under the door. It was a bill for electricity, heat, water, and rental of my room. My dad would call this "making a point."

I took down my sign.

So, this is **my list of excuses** for having a messy room. Some of them work. Sometimes Mom laughs at my excuse, then makes me clean up anyway.

1. Messy Room — No Punishment

David: Would you punish me if I didn't do something?

Mom: No, why?

David: Good, because I didn't clean my room.

[This only works once.]

2. Messy Room — Robber

David: What do you mean, my room's a mess?

Mom: Well, look for yourself.

David: Oh no! I've been robbed!

[Didn't work with Mom. Might work on Dad.]

3. Unmade Bed — Extra Work

Mom: Why didn't you make your bed?

David: I knew I'd just mess it up again when I sleep in it tonight.

[Once I slept on the floor in my sleeping bag for a whole week. This way I didn't have to make my bed every day. I stopped doing it when my dog Boris tried to use my head as a pillow.]

4. <u>Old Lunch in Backpack — Science Experiment</u>

Mom: What's that *ROTTEN LUNCH* doing at the bottom of your backpack?

David: That's my science experiment. Do you think it's ready?

5. <u>Clothes on Floor — Saving Time</u>

Mom: Why are your clothes on the floor?

David: It **saves me time** getting dressed in the morning.

CHAPTER 4

At school, everyone is in charge, except most of the kids, of course.

The crossing guard lady is in charge. She loves blowing her whistle right in your ear if you step into the road too soon.

The *office lady* is in charge (but she's not too bad). She's always making you run a little errand for her. Or getting you to do a little job during lunch. And then, before you know it, lunch is over and it's time to go back to class.

The **principal** is really in charge. He likes to talk and talk and talk. Then sometimes he calls your parents. I try to stay out of his way.

The kids in sixth grade think they're in charge.

They walk around the school making us other kids do things like pick up papers and clean up the hallways. They think they are really cool.

With all those people in charge, it's easy to see why you would need *lots of excuses* at school. If you're out of excuses at school, **you're out of luck.**

| Everyday school excuses |

1. Late Project — Making it Perfect

Rose: Haven't you finished your project yet, Baxter? I handed mine in days ago.

David: Anyone can finish a school project early, Rose. I like to spend as much time as I can on my work before I hand it in.

[Rose Thornton always hands her homework in early. She likes to remind the teacher when the homework is due. Then the rest of us **get into trouble** if we haven't done it. Have I mentioned that *I really, really don't like Rose Thornton?*]

2. Spitball — Physics Problem

Ms. Stacey: David Baxter, was that your spitball that flew past my ear?

David: That wasn't **a spitball**, Ms. Stacey. Joe and I were studying the science of **flying objects**.

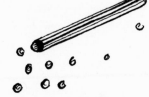

[It helps if you have a piece of paper in front of you with some numbers written on it. I'm not sure what the science of flying objects is, but I'm pretty sure it's got something to do with math.]

3. Recycling Bin — Health Condition

Ms. Stacey: David Baxter, please take the waste paper out to the recycling bin.

David: I'd really like to take the paper out. But I have a serious health condition that makes germs a bad thing to be around.

[Ignore your friend Joe, who suddenly becomes very concerned and wants to know what's wrong.]

4. Lunchtime Detention — Health Condition

Ms. Stacey: All right, David Baxter. No homework means a lunchtime detention for you.

David: But I can't stay inside for lunchtime detention, Ms. Stacey. I have a medical problem that means **my skin** has to be in **the early afternoon sun once a day.**

[I only tried this one once. The thing is, it would have been okay if I'd left it at that. I'd just been reading our medical dictionary at home that morning. I learned a **new medical word** and was ready for anything. So when Ms. Stacey asked me what my medical problem was, I said my *obstetrician* wasn't sure. He was running some tests. Then Ms. Stacey asked me **when my baby was due.** Rose Thornton laughed out loud and her GG's giggled into their pencil cases. That's when I figured I should be **more careful about the medical words** I use. I also figured out I'd be spending my lunchtime in detention.]

5. Reading Work — Contact Lenses

Ms. Stacey: David Baxter, would you like to read what you have written so far?

David Baxter: I can't read my work, Ms. Stacey. I left my contact lenses at home.

[This one almost worked. Just make sure you're not sitting next to Joe Pagnopolous when you use it, because he'll probably offer to READ YOUR WORK FOR YOU. Which is what Joe did. Of course, I hadn't actually written anything down yet. Thanks, Joe.]

6. Not Listening — Distractions

Ms. Stacey: David Baxter, are you listening to me?

David Baxter: I was trying to pay attention, Ms. Stacey! I was just telling Rose Thornton to be quiet because I couldn't hear what you were saying.

[Then frown like you're really annoyed that you missed out on what the teacher is saying. This got me out of being in trouble with Ms. Stacey and got me into being in trouble with Rose Thornton instead. It was worth it.]

CHAPTER 5

THE DOG ATE IT!

This is the **most important section** in my book. Yes, that's right, it's the section about **homework**. Everybody has excuses for why they don't have their homework. Even Rose Thornton has tried some.

There is one thing that you have to understand. **Teachers expect you to have an excuse for not having your homework.** It is the most interesting part of their job. If you can come up with a really good homework excuse, they'll be so impressed that they'll forgive you.

(This didn't work on my teacher last year. She ended up giving me DETENTION and EXTRA HOMEWORK. But it has worked on Ms. Stacey.)

You can't just say you forgot your homework. Even if that is true. Imagine how boring that must be for teachers to hear all the time.

By reading this section, you are actually doing them a favor. (Of course you could always do your **homework** and take it to school, and then you wouldn't even need an EXCUSE. It's up to you.)

1. Locker Stuck

Ms. Stacey: Where is your homework, David?

David: My locker door is stuck and I can't get it out.

[This <u>only</u> works if you have lockers at school.]

2. Silly Dad

Ms. Stacey: Why don't you have your homework today, David?

David: My dad used it to start the FIREPLACE in our living room.

[This works if you have a fireplace in your living room.

It also works if you don't have a fireplace and you're pretty sure that **your teacher will never find out you don't have one.**]

3. Save the Trees

Ms. Stacey: Hand in your homework, please, David.

David: I can't, Ms. Stacey. It's **against my beliefs** to **cut down trees for paper.**

[This worked with one teacher. Another teacher asked me to type my homework into the computer and give her the disk. Ms. Stacey grabbed some paper from the recycling box. Then she made me do my homework on the back of the used paper during lunch. **Not one of my best excuses.**]

4. Throw Up

Ms. Stacey: Where's your homework today, David?

David: My brother **THREW UP** on it.

[This works if you have a younger brother or a teacher who's grossed out by throwing up. It's really good if you go into more detail about the amount of throw up. What it **looked like, smelled like**, that kind of thing. Mention chopped carrots.]

5. Friday the 13th

Ms. Stacey: No homework from you, David?

David: No, Ms. Stacey. It's Friday the 13th. I thought it would be **bad luck** to hand it in today.

[Only works if it is Friday the 13th. This worked once. The other time I was told it was bad luck if I didn't hand it in, and I got extra homework.]

6. Rest

Ms. Stacey: I see you didn't hand your homework in, David.

David: I really wanted to get my homework done. But **Mom** said I need my rest at night.

[This one's worked before. **Mom** is pretty scary, even to teachers. Make sure you don't use it just before school conferences. I did once, and MOM FOUND OUT ABOUT THIS EXCUSE. I ended up having to do my homework as soon as I came home from school. Then I had to go to bed an hour earlier so I could get my rest at night. This went on for a whole month. *Mom just loves making a point.*]

7. Drool

Ms. Stacey: No homework today, David?

David: My brother/sister/dog drooled on it.

[Don't actually say brother sister dog. Just choose one of them. It's helpful if you have a brother or sister or a dog at home.]

8. Disintegrated

Ms. Stacey: Please hand in your science homework, David.

David: My science homework? I'd love to, Ms. Stacey. But, you see, the atomic structure of my paper became unstable, so it **disintegrated.**

[I don't know what this means. My sister, Zoe, got it from a friend who has an older brother who's in college. Ms. Stacey was so impressed with my excuse, she made me write it out a hundred times during recess. I had to look up **a whole lot of words in the dictionary.**]

9. Stolen Backpack

Ms. Stacey: No homework today, David? What a surprise.

David: Don't you want to know what happened, Ms. Stacey?

Ms. Stacey: Sure. *Hit me with your best shot.*

David: It was really scary, Ms. Stacey. Somebody stole my backpack on the way to school.

[This really happened to me. I didn't really have my homework in my backpack at the time. It wasn't a lie because I didn't say I had it. Also, it was my brother, Harry, who stole my bag. I grabbed it back from him right away. But I didn't lie.

When Ms. Stacey made me tell the principal about my stolen backpack, I forgot to mention Harry. And when the principal made me tell the police the story, well, I finally had to tell the whole story. The police didn't really understand that it wasn't technically a lie. They didn't even smile when I said that one day I wanted to be a police officer, just like them.]

CHAPTER 6

LATE FOR SCHOOL

Sometimes, when I'm late for school, I feel like **taking the whole day off.**

Mom thinks if I don't go to school, I'm going to miss out on something really important. Even Dad won't let me stay home.

The trouble with coming to school late is that everyone looks at you like you should be in jail. **The school bully, Victor Sneddon**, is always late. He usually looks like he just got out of bed. Maybe he needs more sleep than the rest of us. **Being a BULLY must take a lot of energy.**

When you come to school late, the teacher writes it down on your report card.

Then your parents look at your report card and ask, *"Why were you late for school seven times this year?"*

(Of course, **it's never my fault**. There are a whole bunch of reasons someone could be late to school.)

This is a good time to tell your parents that you have a problem with someone at school. Or maybe that you're having nightmares. Or that there is something **wrong with your writing hand.**

No matter what you decide to say, just **change the subject.** If you're good enough, they'll forget that you were late to class.

Maybe you shouldn't use the nightmare excuse. I told Mom that one last year and I had to **sleep with a night light for six months**. That wasn't so bad, until Harry told everyone at school about it.

> Anyway, here are some **excuses for being late.**

1. School Sign

Ms. Stacey: Why are you late for school, David?

David: Because of the sign down the road.

Ms. Stacey: What sign?

David: The one that says, **"Slow — School."**

[Okay, this got me a **recess of emptying trash cans**, but a lot of kids laughed. Then, of course, they spent **their** recess not emptying trash cans. I'm not sure it was worth it.]

2. Dog With Rabies

Ms. Stacey: You're late, David.

David: I'm sorry, Ms. Stacey. There was this really BIG DOG and I was too scared to go past it. Actually, it had all **this foam around its mouth**. And its eyes were **really spooky**, like it was in *some kind of a trance*. It was walking funny, with really stiff legs. I'm just glad that cat crossed the road. **Poor cat**. At least it gave me a chance to run, though.

[Sometimes, if you just keep talking, Ms. Stacey gives up and tells you to sit down and start doing some work. The **GG's** were pretty interested in my excuse and asked me at recess for the full story. Rose Thornton just told me I was a weird kid. **"Takes one to know one,"** I answered back. That's always a good reply.]

3. Medical Problem

Ms. Stacey: Does that bandage around your head have anything to do with you being late, David?

David: Well, Mom wasn't going to let me come to school today. **I was up all night with a toothache.** But you know me. I didn't want to miss out on anything.

[Never use if a dentist is in the classroom or anywhere nearby.]

4. Bad Weather

Ms. Stacey: Ah, here at last, Mr. Baxter.

David: Sorry I was late to class, Ms. Stacey, but it was **foggy** (or snowy) and I couldn't find my way to school.

[If you don't walk to school, you could say that the car or bus had to go really slowly because of the fog (or snow). This excuse is good to use during winter, but only if it's actually snowing.]

5. No Milk

Ms. Stacey: Hurry up and sit down, David. You've already missed out on multiplication tables.

David: Sorry I'm late, Ms. Stacey. **There was no milk in the house for cereal** and I had to wait for Mom to go to the grocery store and buy some.

[Try to look as if you're really unhappy that you've just missed multiplication tables. Ignore Rose Thornton asking if you've ever heard of having eggs and toast for breakfast instead of cereal.]

6. Vacuum

Dear Ms. Stacey,

Please excuse David for being late to school today. He left his clothes on his bedroom floor, and my husband <u>sucked them up</u> with the vacuum cleaner. I then had to wash his clothes and iron them before David could come to school.

Yours sincerely,

Cordelia Baxter

[This actually happened. **Really**. But the thing is, Ms. Stacey didn't believe the note was from my mom. She said my dad couldn't be that weird. But Dad can. The thing is, **he was actually reading a book while he was vacuuming**. So then I had to go and sit on the hot seat outside the principal's office. Then Mom found out and she was really angry and Ms. Stacey had to apologize to me. Ms. Stacey was then more scared of my mom and even angrier at me. On second thought, **don't try this excuse**.]

7. Toilet

Ms. Stacey: Late again, David?

David: Sorry I'm late for class, Ms. Stacey. The toilet paper was stuck in the toilet so I pushed it down with my foot. Then my foot got stuck.

[Say this excuse really loudly, so that the girls make lots of disgusted noises. Your teacher will be so busy trying to calm the class down that she'll forget that you were late.

Also, it might help to have a little bit of clean toilet paper stuck to the end of your shoe. Don't really stick your foot down a toilet. It could get MESSY.]

8. Pet Dog

Ms. Stacey: You are twenty minutes late for class, David.

David: I know, Ms. Stacey. But it wasn't my fault. I'm late because **my dog followed me** all the way to school and I had to walk him back home again.

[Of course, my dog, Boris, would never be able to walk all the way to school. It's hard enough just getting him to walk outside for a **bathroom break**.]

9. Stuck in Elevator

Ms. Stacey: What's your excuse for being late this morning, David?

David: Well, I had to deliver something for my mom before school. Then I got stuck in an elevator.

I used the **elevator phone**, but no one answered. I had to wait until 9 a.m. until **someone came to rescue me.**

[This one sounds real, but it never actually happened. I almost got away with this one, but Rose Thornton had to say, "Which elevator? What building?" Then Ms. Stacey looked like she wanted an answer to Rose's question. I remembered that I'd read about a sickness where people are scared of being in small spaces. So I said that I had **arachnophobia**, which made it even worse to be stuck in a tiny elevator. Then Ms. Stacey asked if there was a spider in the elevator with me.

I realized that arachnophobia was actually **the fear of spiders**, not of **being in small spaces**. So then I pretended to faint. And the whole time Rose Thornton was saying, "He's faking it. He is so just faking it." If you're going to use this excuse, don't mention phobias at all.]

10. Car Wash

Ms. Stacey: You're late, David. And you're soaking wet.

David: Sorry, Ms. Stacey, but Mom drove through a car wash and **our car got stuck**. We had to wait there for hours. Then Mom made me get out of the car to go push the emergency stop button. So, that's why I'm late and wet.

Ms. Stacey: Amazing, David.

[The real story? I was walking to school. The night before there had been a **big rainstorm**. There were lots of puddles around and I stopped to make a paper boat to float on a puddle. Then someone **bet me** that I **couldn't jump over a really huge puddle**. So I tried to jump, but I slipped right into the puddle. I don't know if Ms. Stacey believed my story, but she did suggest that I use the idea for the short story I had to write that day.]

CHAPTER 7

PLEASE EXCUSE JOE'S ABSENCE

I don't mind school most of the time. But sometimes I just need a break, like my friend **Joe Pagnopolous.**

Joe's family owns a $VIDEO$ $STORE$. Joe has a very cool mom. If Joe doesn't feel like going to school, his mom usually lets him stay home. The problem is, Joe has to have all his homework done before he can stay home. And when he stays home, he has to help his parents at their store. He has to rewind the video tapes, clean the video and DVD covers, and put stickers on all the things for sale. I don't know why he doesn't stay home more often.

When Joe stays home, his mother writes a note for the teacher. The note always says the same thing.

Dear Ms. Stacey,

Please excuse Joe's absence. He was sick of school for the day.

Yours truly,

Mia Pagnopolous

Joe **never** gives these notes to his teachers. He knows that they will just flip out if they read such a thing. So, over the years, Joe and I have worked on some excuses that the teachers will be happy with.

The thing about writing **excuses from parents** is that you have to TYPE THEM or else the teacher will **recognize your handwriting. Also, you can't have any spelling mistakes.**

Here are some of the **best excuses we've come up with.**

1. Old Newspaper

Dear Ms. Stacey,

Please excuse Joe for missing school yesterday. We have the Sunday paper delivered every weekend. We forgot to pick up our Sunday paper on Sunday.

When we found it on Monday, we thought it was Sunday, so Joe didn't come to school.

Yours sincerely,

Mia Pagnopolous

2. Pajamas

Dear Ms. Stacey,

Please excuse Joe's absence. Joe walks to school. He was halfway to school when he realized he forgot to put on his jeans. By the time he walked back home, I had put his clothes into the wash and he didn't have anything to wear except for his pajamas. It is against our religion to go to school in pajamas. I hope you understand.

Yours truly,

Mia Pagnopolous

3. Eye test

Dear Ms. Stacey,

Please excuse Joe for missing school yesterday.
He had an <u>optimism</u> appointment and should be
seeing things better soon.

Yours truly,

Mia Pagnopolous

[We meant to say **optometrist** appointment,
but I don't think Ms. Stacey noticed that we used the
wrong word.]

CHAPTER 8

BULLY FOR YOU

I don't care what teachers might think, there's a bully in every school. (Look under the entry for VICTOR SNEDDON at the beginning of this book.) Usually there's **a major school bully** that everyone knows about. Everyone knows the rules for a bully. Keep away from this person. Don't make this person mad. If you do, say that it's all your fault and back away slowly. **Don't look this person in the eye.** Don't make any sudden movements. And don't give them any excuses at all.

There are also the kids who take turns being the school bully for the day. It is worth using an excuse on these kids. It's good if you have friends to help you out. Discuss different ideas with them before you need to use an excuse for a bully. **It just might save your life.**

Let's say you're in the schoolyard and you just did something that annoyed a bully. The bully has you backed into a corner. There's no way out.

The only teacher you can see is taking care of a problem at the other end of the schoolyard.

1. Wanted by the Principal

Get your friend to walk over and talk to you.

Joe: Hey, David. The principal wants you in his office. Looks like you're really in trouble this time.

[This is a perfect excuse for getting out of a bully's way. Not only do you have an excuse, but **the bully will be impressed that you are in trouble with the principal.** The only trouble with this is that the bully may want to talk to you later to find out why you were in trouble.]

2. Meeting with Another Bully

David: I'd like to stay and talk about what I did that annoyed you. But if I don't get back to Victor Sneddon in the **next thirty seconds** with some lunch, he's going to come looking for me.

And if he finds out you're the reason I didn't get back to him, well, **let's just say, I wouldn't want to be you.**

[If there's one thing you can rely on, it's that a bully can usually be scared by another bully. Except if it's Victor Sneddon, of course. He can never be scared.]

3. Just Fake It

David: I blacked out. **What happened?**

[You can use this one if you happen to get in the way of a bully's game, and you caused the bully to lose. It looks real if you fall down on the ground and close your eyes for a second. **Be careful not to stay on the ground for too long.** You don't want the bully standing over you.]

4. Just Tricking

David: A fight? You want to have a fight? Gee, I'd love to. But I'm *allergic to violence.* Just ask my older, larger brother. He's standing behind you.

[As the bully looks behind him, run as fast as you can. In fact, RUN FASTER.]

5. Gross Out

David: You want to take my lunch? Sure. My mom makes the best tuna and jam sandwich ever.

[Then look around in the bottom of your lunch bag and pretend that you can't find the sandwich. This usually makes the bully go away. If not, you can always keep a tuna and jam sandwich in the bottom of your bag for emergencies.]

6. Who, Me?

One day some kid heard that I had said something mean about him. I didn't even know the guy, let alone what his name was. I think maybe Rose started the rumor just to get me into trouble. Anyway, my meeting with the bully went something like this:

Bully: Are you David Baxter?

David: David Baxter? No, I'm not David Baxter. Some people say we look alike. I hear he's a real loser.

Then I just walked away, shaking my head as if the last person in the world I'd want to be is the person that the bully is looking for. **Which was actually true**.

7. Do I Know You?

I used this excuse one day when a bully found me drinking out of his water bottle during gym class.

It wasn't my fault. **All water bottles look the same.** Just because his bottle is blue and mine is red, and just because I'd left my bottle at home, doesn't mean I did it ON PURPOSE. I just forgot I didn't have my bottle with me. But when he told me he was going to get me after school, I knew I was in trouble.

So Bec and I planned a really good excuse. When Bec and I walked past the oak tree after school, the bully jumped out in front of me. "DO I know you?" I asked him.

Then Bec explained to him that I had recently been in a terrible accident and I had lost my memory.

I tried to look pale and serious.

"It's sad," said Bec. **"His memory is almost completely gone."**

I looked at Bec. "Do I know you?" I asked.

"Just stay away from my water bottle," said the bully as he walked away, shaking his head.

[I would only try this if you have a friend like Bec to help you out. That girl can tell stories better than I can when she wants to.]

CHAPTER 9

WHAT ADULTS REALLY MEAN

I got the idea for this chapter from Joe. When we were talking about writing this book, he said, "Have you ever noticed that adults can get away with **really dumb excuses?"**

I hadn't really paid attention before, but after that I started to.

Adults are FULL OF EXCUSES. Take Dad, for instance. Instead of saying he didn't want to spend a boring hour looking at Mr. McCafferty's world stamp collection, Dad pretended that his glasses were broken. The thing is, my dad doesn't wear glasses.

Then there's my sister, Zoe, who's kind of an adult. (She's a teenager, which is almost the same thing.) Zoe gets out of going to boring parties by saying, **"Something's come up."** She never really explains what actually came up. It makes her seem MYSTERIOUS at the same time.

Just imagine me trying to use that excuse on Bec Trigg. She'd want to know WHAT had come up, what, when, where and why. There's no way I could use that excuse with Bec.

It seems to me that adults get to use a **whole lot of excuses that kids can never use.**

I'd Love to, But . . .

When I was Harry's age, I thought that it would be great to be older. Being an adult meant **driving a car, staying up as late as you wanted,** and **not having to do things you didn't want to do.** If you didn't feel like going to someone's place for dinner, you didn't have to.

"Hi, Joe, just letting you know that I don't feel like coming over for dinner tonight."

"No problemo, David. See you later."

"See you, Joe."

Of course, now I know that **being an adult isn't as easy as that**. If you don't want to do something, you'd better have an excuse not to do it. It's not good manners otherwise.

1. Diet

Mom: Oh, I'd love to come for dinner, but my doctor's put me on a *clean liver diet*. I should be eating normally in a few months.

[Mom used this excuse to get out of eating at Dad's Aunt Meg's house. Aunt Meg's husband used to be a butcher and Aunt Meg is really big on offal. Offal is the stuff from an animal that you shouldn't eat. Stuff like TONGUE and BRAINS and LIVER. I used to think it was called awful, because I think it is. Awful, that is. Anyway, even Dad hates eating at Aunt Meg's house. "I'm not eating anything that someone's been thinking with," Dad likes saying. It's enough to make you a vegetarian.]

2. Thanks, But No Thanks

Dad: I'm sure the family would love to come for lunch, Zandra. But, I'll be away for work that weekend, so *you won't see me.*

[Mom's got a vegetarian friend named Zandra Zen. They use to go to school together. In fact, Mom got her famous vegetarian loaf recipe from Zandra. Zandra Zen wasn't always her name. Dad said he knew her back in the old days when she used to be plain old Sandra Brown. Anyway, Zandra wears **really strange clothes** with **moons** and STARS and STRIPES and **dots**. Her hair is purple and she cooks food made out of this white stuff called **tofu** that **tastes like nothing**. Dad doesn't mind Zandra, but he definitely doesn't like going to her place to eat. When we go there to eat, I always ask if Boris can come so that I can feed him my food under the table. Tofu and beans and brown rice. It's enough to make you eat offal.]

3. Gotta Work

Dad: Honey, I'd love to come to the flower show with you, but I'm behind with my work. You go and have a good time though.

[The weird thing is, Dad uses this excuse with Mom **every year** and they both know that it is an excuse. I've never seen Dad bring his work home, though sometimes he'll sit at his computer and look busy. Harry and I think that he just plays games on the computer. Anyway, Dad gets to stay home and Mom gets to enjoy her flower show, so it's **an excuse that works for both of them.**]

4. Sorry, I Didn't See You

Zoe practically **lives at the shopping mall.** Zoe and her friends like to stand around and look in the store windows and check out who's at the mall.

Now, there's no way anyone can **not** see my mom if she wants you to. I've seen her in action and it's pretty impressive. My mom can grab the attention of someone at the juice counter halfway across the mall by just waving her arms around and SHOUTING. I know this, because that's what she did to me. I tried to ignore her. Then some other customer at the mall said to her friend, "There's a crazy woman yelling at you. Something about orange juice or pineapple. **Should I call security?**"

Of course Zoe would have seen Mom if she was at the mall, too. But Zoe is too cool to look like she might have a mother, let alone talk to her. So Zoe's excuse is:

Zoe: Were you at the mall today, Mom? Sorry, I didn't see you.

CHAPTER 10

Some adults pretend to be something they're not, and use this as an excuse for not doing something they don't want to do. **Here are some examples.**

1. Hearing Trouble

Gran: What? Sorry, I can't hear you.

[Gran's pretty smart, but sometimes she puts on this old lady act. Her favorite excuse is that she's old. If she doesn't want to answer a question, or do something, she'll **pretend she can't hear**. I've seen her pretend to be asleep at the dinner table when it's time to do the dishes. It's not like Mom's going to make her do the dishes, but Gran pretends anyway. I know it's an act. And she knows that I know it's an act. But for some reason, I never tell Mom that I know. Sometimes, being a really old person is just as hard as being a kid.]

2. Speak Greek

Mrs. Pagnopolous: I no speak English.

[Joe's mom can speak **English** perfectly. She can also speak GREEK and GERMAN. She used to teach language before she and Mr. P. bought the video store. Joe's mom was born in this country. So was her husband. They have relatives that came from Greece a long time ago, so they can both speak Greek. Mrs. P. sounds just like my mom, but when she doesn't want to speak to someone, *she'll pretend she can't understand them.* This worked once when a police officer tried to give her a traffic ticket. She just WAVED Joe and me into her car while talking in Greek to the parking officer. He gave up before long and **she drove away without getting a ticket.**

Just remember my **disclaimer** at the beginning of the book!]

3. I'm Confused

Dad: Oh, the meeting was last Sunday? I thought you said **this** Sunday.

[Dad is some kind of scientist. I'm not quite sure what he does, but he wears a white coat at work and there are microscopes and stuff. Anyway, **Dad likes to pretend he's really forgetful.**  He's so good at pretending that anyone who knows him just thinks he's some kind of nutty professor. I've seen him get out of meetings, Scout picnics, and taking kids to practice. He **can't forget Mom's birthday**, though. There is no excuse for that.]

CHAPTER 11

WOULD YOU BELIEVE...

Some adults use excuses that no kid would even dare to try. I mean, you really **wonder how they get away with it sometimes.**

1. Sorry to Disturb You

Mr. McCafferty: Mrs. Baxter, good evening. I'm sorry to call you. But it's about David.

[Mr. McCafferty likes to talk. Mom says she feels sorry for him because he lives alone in his house with just his cat, **Mr. Figgins,** to talk to. Mr. McCafferty would never just call my parents for no reason, so **he always uses me as an excuse.** Sometimes he'll spend so long on the phone that my mom can clean the house, cook dinner, and give Boris a bath before Mr. McCafferty hangs up. Mom says it's lucky that we have a cordless phone, because otherwise she would never get anything done.]

2. You Must Be Mistaken

Ms. Stacey: This poster of Smashing Smorgan? *Of course it's not mine.* I took it away from one of the students in this class.

[Ms. Stacey is crazy about **Smashing Smorgan**, but she spends a lot of time pretending that she's not. I'm sure it would be easier if she would just admit she is. Then she could put her Smashing Smorgan poster on the wall behind her desk and we could all enjoy it.]

3. Broken Washing Machine

Please excuse Bec from gym class today because she does not have her uniform. Our washing machine is broken.

Sincerely,

Bronte Trigg

[Bec's mom is really nice, but she's not like any other moms I know. For one thing, I call her **Bronte**, because she hates being called anything else.

Bec's mom is an artist, which means that sometimes Bec won't have dinner until 9 p.m. Sometimes Bec **can stay up really late** because her mom will forget that Bec didn't go to bed.

When Bronte is in the middle of a project, **she forgets about everything**. Including CLEAN school clothes.]

℣. The Check's in the Mail

Bronte Trigg: Of course I've paid that bill. The check's in the mail.

[As I said, Bronte's really not that organized. Sometimes she FORGETS about the bills stuck on the fridge until she gets a call saying that she owes money. Then she says that the check is already in the mail. **She always blames the post office** for the check getting lost or taking too long to arrive. I've heard a lot of people use this excuse. **I'd sure hate to be a mailman.**]

5. I Didn't Recognize You

Mom: Oh goodness. Sorry, I wasn't ignoring you. I just didn't realize it was you.

[This is Mom's excuse when she has been caught trying to avoid someone. Mom's really weird about going to the grocery store in her old garden clothes. But sometimes she races down to the store and hopes that no one she knows will see her. Of course, someone usually does. Once I found her **hiding in the pet food section of the supermarket** because she'd spotted Mr. McCafferty in the next aisle. She snuck out to the car hiding behind a couple of boxes of cat food. The thing is, we don't have a cat.]

6. I've Already Got One

Dad: I've already got one. Goodbye.

[Dad uses this excuse a lot. He uses it on people who call during dinner and want to **sell something**.

He's used it on the vacuum cleaner salesperson at the shopping mall. And on the kids who come around trying to sell GIRL SCOUT COOKIES. And on the person who wanted some answers for a survey. He even used it on some strange people who came to our front door trying to sell us a ticket to the kingdom of heaven. I think they were impressed he already had a ticket, because they left pretty quickly.]

7. Let's Just Stay Friends

Zoe: I can't possibly go out with you. **We're friends.** Let's say we went out. Maybe we'd like it. So then we'd go out again. And maybe we'd like it even more. So then, what if my friends found out we were going out? Then they'd start asking me whether you were my **boyfriend or not**. And then they'd start picking on the way you look, or dress, or talk, or something. And then I'd look at you and think, "Hey, maybe they're right." So then I'd want to break up with you and you'd get **all hurt** and probably say STUFF to your friends.

And then maybe your friends would start a rumor. And then things would really get ugly and we wouldn't be talking anymore. After being such good friends! Wouldn't it be disappointing if that happened? I care too much about our friendship. So you see, I can't possibly go out with you.

[This is the **longest excuse** I have ever heard. BEC and JOE and I listened to Zoe on the phone once and this is exactly what she said. We know that for a fact, because Joe was pretending to be some **famous detective** and he had a tape recorder with him so we taped it. Bec thought that maybe Zoe could grow up to be a famous politician one day. Joe thought that wouldn't work, because Zoe cares too much about what other people think. But Bec said, "Don't you get it? She never wanted to date the guy in the first place!"

Joe and I still didn't get it. "Wouldn't it be easier to just say NO?" asked Joe. I had to agree.]

CHAPTER 12

FINALLY

Well, those are ALL THE EXCUSES I have time for now. I hope there's an excuse in this book that helps make your life easier.

My friend Joe Pagnopolous read most of this book and he wanted me to mention him some more, so I just did. Hi, Joe.

Rose Thornton found out I was writing this book even though it was supposed to be a secret.

"I hope you're not putting me in another book, Baxter," she said with a frown.

Bec Trigg said that this book **will never get published.**

"Adults aren't going to like a book about excuses for kids," she said.

"Who says it's just for kids?" I asked. Bec admitted I had a point.

I've decided I'm going to give Mom my **Excuses** book for a **present on her next birthday.** I bet she'll like it even more than "1001 Handy Hints for Homemakers."

I've read over everything I've written in this book and it made me realize a FEW THINGS.

1. Boris is still **never going to win** a dog show competition.

2. Tuna and jam sandwiches **really aren't too bad.**

3. Using excuses can sometimes get you into **more trouble** than you were in before you used them.

But hey, how was I supposed to know? I'm just a kid.

That's MY EXCUSE, and **I'm sticking to it.**

The End

About the Author

When Karen Tayleur was growing up, her father told
her many stories about his own childhood. These stories
continued to grow. She says, "I always enjoyed the
retelling, and wanted to create a character who had
the same abilities with 'bending the truth.'" And David
Mortimore Baxter was born! Karen lives in Australia
with her husband, two children, two cats, and one dog.

About the Illustrator

Brann Garvey grew up in the great state of Iowa, where
he studied art and visual communications. He graduated
from the Minneapolis College of Art & Design with a
degree in illustration. Brann is usually found with one or
more of the following: a pencil in his hand, a comic book,
a remote for watching DVDs, or his pet kitty, Iggy. When
the weather is nice, Brann likes to play disc golf, and he
proudly points out that Iowa is one of the world's centers
for the sport. Iggy does not play.

Glossary

annoy (uh-NOI)—to bother someone

atomic structure (uh-TOM-ik STRUK-chur)—how an object is put together with all of its atoms

detention (di-TEN-shuhn)—to stay after school for punishment

disintegrated (diss-IN-tuh-grate-id)—broken into lots of small pieces

errand (ER-uhnd)—a short trip to send a message or pick something up

excuse (ek-SKYOOSS)—a reason why something was not done, or why something was done the wrong way

offal (AW-ful)—the parts of an animal that are usually not eaten, such as the tongue and brains

physics (FIZ-iks)—the science of physical objects and energy (such as light, sound, and electricity)

rabies (RAY-beez)—a disease of warm-blooded animals such as dogs

succeed (suk-SEED)—to do something well

survive (sur-VIVE)—to stay alive

tofu (TOE-foo)—a soft, white food made from soybeans

Discussion Questions

1. The subtitle of this book is "Survive and Succeed with David Mortimore Baxter." Did David's excuses help him survive? Did they help him succeed? Use examples from the book to explain your answers.

2. Compare what David says he's figured out at the beginning of the book (see page 10) versus what he has figured out by the end of the book (see page 71). How has he changed? Why?

3. Are you familiar with any of the excuses that were mentioned in this book? Have you tried any of them? What excuses of your own have you used? Discuss how your excuses have worked or not worked.

4. What do you think is the point of this book?

Writing Prompts

1. David mentions lots of characters in this book. Did any character remind you of yourself? Write about how and why you identified with a certain character.

2. At the end of the book, David uses the excuse "I'm just a kid." Have you ever used that excuse to get out of anything? Did it work or not? Write about it.

3. Write your own list of excuses for situations you've been in and needed an excuse for. Can you come up with some better excuses than David did?

4. David says that his mother has "eyes in the back of her head." What does this mean? Write about someone you know who watches you with "eyes" like that. Who are they? Why are they always watching you?

MORE fun

David Mortimore Baxter

David is a great kid, but he has one big problem—he can't stop talking. These wildly humorous stories, told by David himself, will show readers just how much trouble a boy and his mouth can get into, whether he's making promises to become class president or bragging that he's best friends with the world's most famous wrestler. David is amiable, engaging, cool, and smart enough to realize that growing up is the biggest adventure of all.

with David!

Promises!
DAVID
MORTIMORE
BAXTER

THE SECRET LIFE OF DAVID MORTIMORE BAXTER

secrets! DAVID MORTIMORE BAXTER
by KAREN TAYLEUR

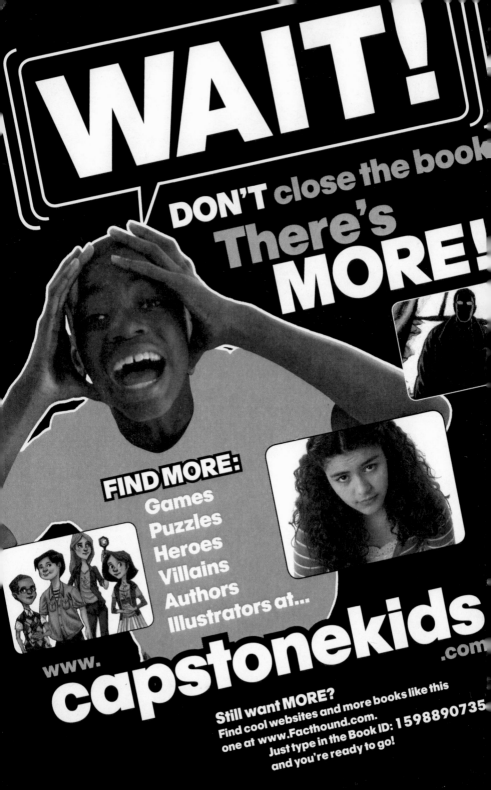